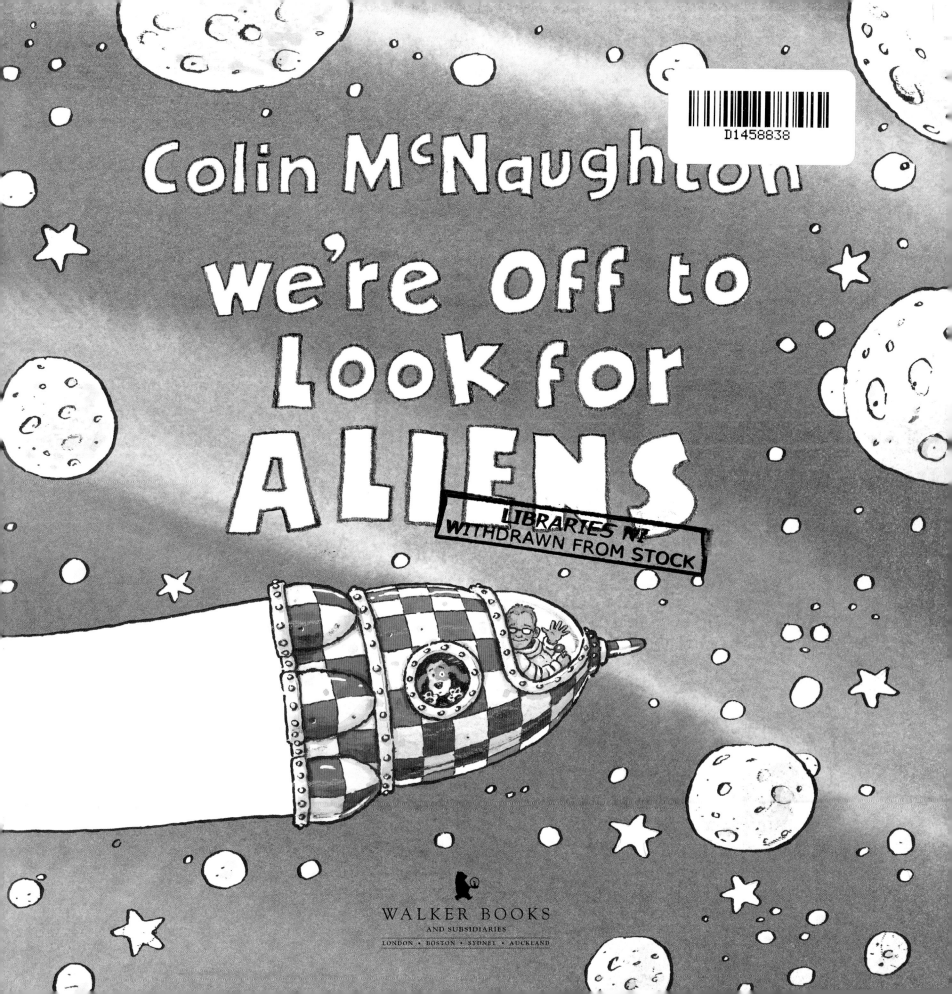

Colin McNaughton

We're off to Look for ALIENS

WALKER BOOKS
AND SUBSIDIARIES
LONDON · BOSTON · SYDNEY · AUCKLAND

"Ah-ha!" said Dad.
"My alien book. Thank you,
Mister Postman."

It was Dad's new book, fresh from the printer. Dad writes children's books. He also does the pictures. He says it's hard work – although he seems to spend an awful lot of time messing about.

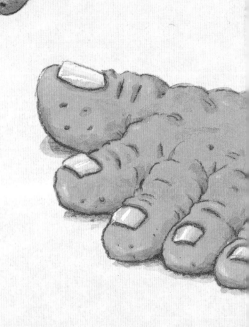

"Tell me what you think,"
said Dad, handing us the book.
"I hope you like it."

Dad said he was too nervous
to watch us read, so he took
the dog for a walk.

This is what we read

We're off to look for aliens,
Ugly-bugly aliens,
We're off to look for aliens,
Wilberforce and I.

We built a little rocket ship,
A rocket ship, a pocket ship.
We built a little rocket ship,
Wilberforce and I.

To all our friends we said, "Goodbye."
Said, "Goodbye, we must fly."
We blasted off into the sky,
Wilberforce and I.

Around the moon and to the stars,
To the stars! To the stars!
We landed on the planet Mars,
Wilberforce and I.

Planet Mars was hot and dry,
We looked a Martian in the eye.
We said hello and said goodbye,
Wilberforce and I.

"Here we go round the universe,
The universe, the universe.
Here we go round the universe,
Wilberforce and I."

These beings came in different sizes,
Different guises, different sizes.
We were in for some surprises,
Wilberforce and I.

We saw lots of smelly things,
Never-seen-on-telly things.
Eyeballs-in-their-belly things,
Wilberforce and I.

Some were cold and some were hot,
Some were tall and some were squat.
We were friendly (they were not!),
Wilberforce and I.

We weren't welcome anywhere
And we were running out of air.
Just one more planet – over there,
Wilberforce and I.

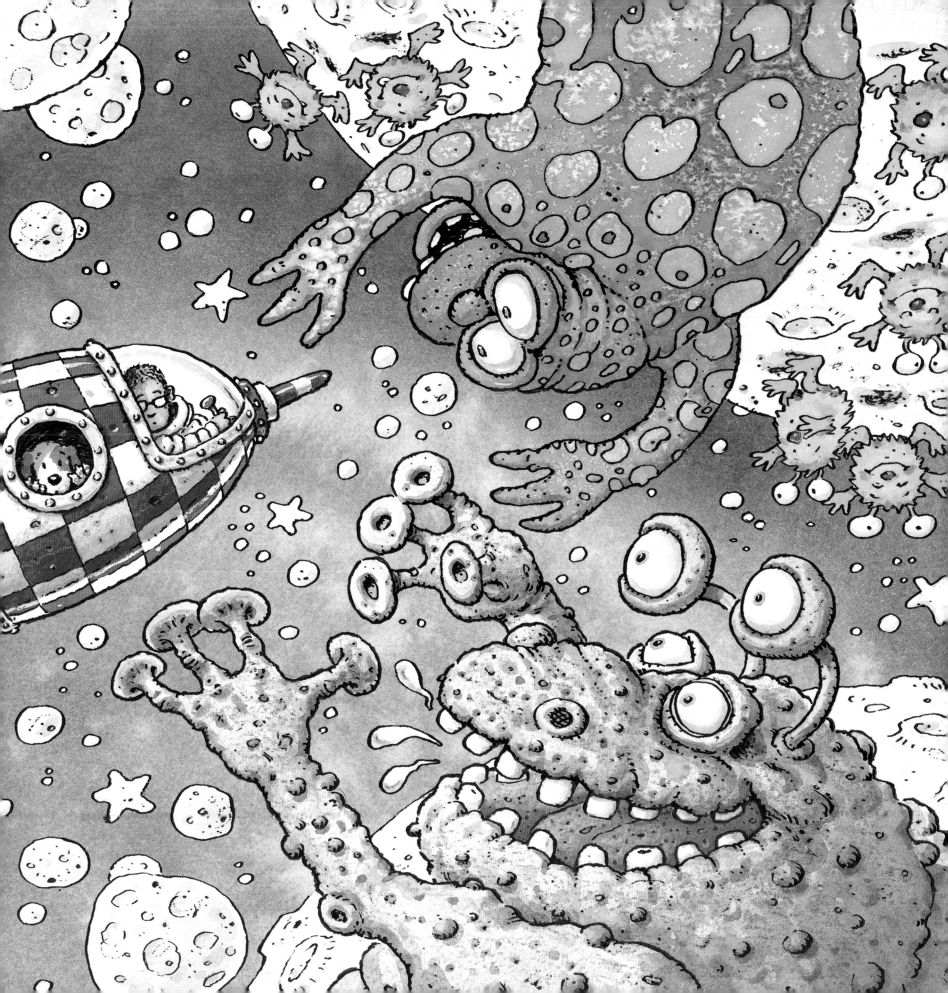

There we met an alien girl,
An alien girl, an alien girl.
We met a lovely alien girl,
Wilberforce and I.

I fell in love and took her home,
Took her home, took her home.
We blasted off and took her home,
Wilberforce and I.

We landed safely, hip-hooray!
Hip-hooray! Hip-hooray!
A little bump, but all okay,
Wilberforce, the alien girl and I.

And we were happy ever after,
Full of laughter, ever after.
We were happy ever after –
in a whirl,
my alien girl.
What a joy,
a baby boy.
Then another,
baby brother.
And of course,
Wilberforce – and I.

THE END

Praise for *We're Off To Look For Aliens*:

"Out of this world!"
Books for Kiddywinks

"This one should rocket up
the bestseller charts."
Fireworks Weekly

"Colin McNaughton is wonderful!"
His Mum

"Well," said Dad, back from his walk,
"what do you think of my alien book?"
"It's brilliant, Dad," said my
brother. "But there's a problem."
"What sort of problem?" frowned Dad.
"Well," said Mum carefully. "It's a
great book and kids will love the pictures,

but ... it's the story."
"What's wrong with it?" said Dad.
"It's a wonderful story!"
"Yes, Dad," I said. "We agree.
It's just that children like
fairy tales and stuff, and
we were wondering, Dad ...

Other books by
Colin McNaughton

Who's That Banging on the Ceiling?
ISBN 978-1-4063-4736-4

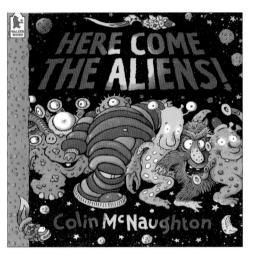

Here Come the Aliens!
ISBN 978-0-7445-4394-0

**Have You Seen Who's Just Moved
In Next Door to Us?**
ISBN 978-1-4063-4737-1

Giant
ISBN 978-1-4063-4738-8

Available from all good booksellers

www.walker.co.uk